Daniel's Pet

Green Light Readers
Harcourt, Inc.
San Diego   New York   London

Daniel's Pet

Alma Flor Ada

Illustrated by G. Brian Karas

Requests for permission to make copies of any part of the work should be
mailed to the following address: Permissions Department, Harcourt, Inc.,
6277 Sea Harbor Drive, Orlando, Florida 32887-6777.

www.HarcourtBooks.com

First Green Light Readers edition 2002
Green Light Readers is a trademark of Harcourt, Inc.,
registered in the United States of America and/or other jurisdictions.

Library of Congress Cataloging-in-Publication Data
Ada, Alma Flor.
Daniel's pet/Alma Flor Ada; illustrated by G. Brian Karas.
p. cm.
Summary: A young boy takes good care of his pet chicken,
and when she is grown up she gives him a surprise.
[1. Chickens—Fiction. 2. Pets—Fiction.] I. Karas, G. Brian, ill. II. Title.
PZ7.A1857Dap 2002
[E]—dc21 2001007732
ISBN 0-15-204577-5
ISBN 0-15-204576-7 pb

A C E G H F D B
A C E G H F D B (pb)

To Cristina Isabel, who loves Daniel.
With love from Abuelita
—A. F. A.

Daniel held a small baby chick.

It was soft in his hands.

"Can I have her as a pet?"
"Yes, Daniel," said Mama.

"I'll call her Jen," said Daniel.

Daniel fed Jen.

Daniel fed all the hens.

Daniel fed Jen every day.

Jen got very big.

One day, Daniel didn't see Jen.
"Jen! Jen!" Daniel called.

"Jen is in here," said Mama.
"Look at her eggs."

"Oh my!" said Daniel.
"Now I will have lots of pets!"

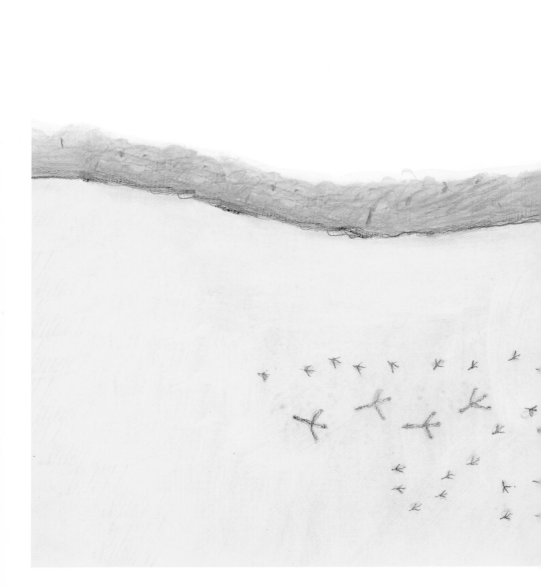

Meet the Author and Illustrator

Alma Flor Ada has always loved to write about nature. As a child, she spent hours near a river watching plants, insects, birds, and frogs. Now she lives in a small house near a lake, where she still enjoys watching the natural world.

Brian Karas lives near many farms. He thought about the chickens he sees on those farms as he drew the pictures for Daniel's Pet.